AMIRAH HILL

BOOK SPINE PUBLISHING LTD.

Copyright © 20204

All rights reserved.
No part of this book may be used or reproduced by any means, graphic, electronic, or mechanical, including photocopying, recording, taping or by any information storage retrieval system without the written permission of the author except in the case of brief quotations embodied in critical articles and reviews.
The views expressed in this work are solely those of the author and do not necessarily reflect the views of the publisher, and the publisher hereby disclaims any responsibility for them.
No part of this book may be reproduced in any form or by any electronic or mechanical means including information storage and retrieval systems, without permission, in writing from the author. The only exception is by the reviewer, who may quote short excerpts in a review.
Any people depicted in stock imagery provided by Thinkstock are models, and such images are being used for illustrative purposes only. Certain stock imagery @Thinkstock.
ISBN Paperback:

life difficult, especially for the children. Her presence cast a dark shadow over the orphanage, and no one liked her—except for a few staff members who followed her orders to keep their jobs. Two staff workers secretly despised Ms. Haasmaun's cruelty, but they remained silent, fearful of losing their positions.

Their families depended on the income, and they couldn't afford to risk it. For the boys, especially Michael and Louie, Ms. Haasmaun was a source of constant dread. Many nights they would whisper their one shared wish: for her to leave and never return. Little did they know, their wish might just come true by the end of their story. Sofia, the bright light in their bleak world, only worked during the day and evenings, never staying overnight.

She volunteered out of love for the boys, always going the extra mile to make their lives a little brighter. But her warmth and kindness didn't go unnoticed by Ms. Haasmaun, who disliked Sofia's gentle approach. The headmistress often picked on her, frustrated by Sofia's refusal to treat the children with the same harshness she herself did. However, Ms. Haasmaun had no power over Sofia's position—Sofia came from a wealthy, influential family, and even the headmistress couldn't force her to leave.

This was the daily routine for Michael, Louie, and the other boys. At 6 a.m., they rose from their beds, made them neatly, took quick showers, and got dressed. By 7 a.m., they were eating breakfast, and by 8 a.m., school began. Lunch came at noon, followed by more schoolwork until 3 p.m. After school, the boys returned to their chores—cleaning, yard work, and tidying up the living quarters. Dinner was served at 6 p.m., followed by a brief period of playtime until 8 p.m., when the boys would start preparing for bed. By 8:30 p.m., the lights were out, and the orphanage fell into silence.
Michael and Louie shared beds right next to each other, their proximity providing them with a small sense of comfort in an otherwise cold world. On weekends, their schedules loosened slightly with more playtime, though Sundays were reserved for church services, followed by free time for the rest of the day.

Holidays at the orphanage, however, were a grim affair. While other children celebrated with laughter and joy, the boys' holidays were often dull and uneventful. Their teacher, Mr. Hagsworth, was no better than Ms. Haasmaun. Tall and thin with jet black hair, bushy eyebrows, and sharp brown eyes, he was notorious for his strictness. His pointy nose and eagle-like gaze

Though life at the orphanage was tough, with strict staff members and few moments of kindness, Michael and Louie found joy in their friendship and their shared love of snow, winter, and music. Their one wish was to be adopted together into a loving family, escaping the harsh realities of the orphanage for a better life.

One bright spot in their lives was Sofia, an 18-year-old girl who worked at the orphanage. With her long brownish-blonde hair, bright blue eyes, and warm smile, she radiated kindness. Though she came from a wealthy family that owned several properties in Manhattan, Sofia chose to volunteer at the orphanage, driven by a deep love for children. She had been working there for over a year and quickly formed a special bond with Michael and Louie, becoming the big sister they had always longed for.
Sofia's kindness knew no bounds—she often snuck them candies, chocolates, and small toys, bringing a bit of light into their difficult lives. Michael and Louie adored her, and in return, she treated them as though they were her own brothers.

The orphanage itself was a sprawling two-story building with a vast courtyard where the children would play on weekends and during their free time. Behind the courtyard stood the boys' school, a separate two-story structure where they spent their days learning and studying. There was also a small infirmary for when one of the boys fell ill. The orphanage's living quarters were divided into two wings, each housing 20 boys and three staff members.
The front of the building featured a large living room, a recreation area, and a spacious kitchen. The staff lived in three bedrooms, with the headmistress occupying the largest suite.

As Michael and Louie gazed out at the snowy courtyard, they dreamed of a brighter future—a future where they could leave the orphanage together and build a life filled with adventure, music, and love. And though they didn't know what lay ahead, they held on to hope, with Sofia by their side, making each day a little more bearable in their kingdom of snow.

The orphanage was ruled with an iron fist by the headmistress, Ms. Haasmaun. At 50 years old, she had a heart as cold as the New York winter and reveled in her position of power. She made sure everyone knew who was in charge, often going out of her way to remind the staff and boys that she controlled everything. Ms. Haasmaun's obsession with money and luxury overshadowed any trace of kindness. She seemed to take pleasure in making

SNOWKINGDOM

On a chilly December 23, 1950, in the heart of New York City, nestled among the bustling streets, stood an orphanage. This was home to 40 boys, each with a story marked by loss or hardship. Some had lost their parents, while others had been placed there because their families could no longer care for them. Among them were two inseparable best friends whose bond transcended the tough circumstances they found themselves in.

One of them was Michael Kelly, a 10-year-old Irish boy with striking green eyes, a cascade of freckles, and a head full of brown hair. His fair complexion often gave him a rosy-cheeked appearance. At just 4 feet 6 inches, Michael was small for his age but filled with dreams far bigger than his stature. His parents, Irish immigrants, had passed away when he was only three, victims of a cruel illness that took them far too soon. Despite his tragic past, Michael found solace in his love for trains, stories, music, and baseball. He dreamed of one day becoming a train conductor and admired the legendary Babe Ruth, often imagining himself as Ruth, stepping up to bat for the New York Yankees.

His best friend, Louie Jones, was the same age but came from a different world. A native New Yorker, Louie was an African American boy with big, soulful brown eyes and a head of tight, curly hair. His parents, struggling to make ends meet, had left him at the orphanage when he was just a year old, hoping to give him a chance at a better life. Louie shared Michael's love for baseball, but his true passion was jazz. He adored Louis Armstrong and dreamed of becoming a jazz band leader, pretending to be Armstrong during their playtime, so much so that everyone affectionately called him "Little Louie Armstrong."

made him intimidating, and he had a habit of reporting any minor infraction to Ms. Haasmaun. She would then dole out harsh punishments, isolating the boys or assigning them extra chores to complete. But two days before Christmas, something magical seemed to fill the air. The boys had just finished their school day and rushed to the courtyard to play games. Michael and Louie, as usual, teamed up for a game of baseball. Michael beamed as he gripped the bat, shouting, "Here I am, Babe Ruth! I'm going to be the greatest baseball player ever!" Sure enough, their team triumphed with a score of 7 to 1.

As dusk fell, the boys were called inside for dinner. After the meal, they cleaned the dining room and kitchen, each boy assigned to a different chore. At 6:30 p.m., it was finally playtime again. Louie darted to the record player and put on a Louis Armstrong record, filling the room with the sweet sounds of jazz. As the music played, Louie began to sing, mimicking Armstrong's voice as best he could. "How about that, buddy?" Louie asked Michael after the song ended. "I'm going to be just like him when I grow up. He's the best, my favorite person in the world. One day, I'll be leading a big band just like Louis Armstrong!" Michael grinned and replied, "Yes, and you and I will be famous! We'll have fun, live near each other, and be brothers forever."
"You're already like my brother, Michael," Louie said, his smile wide. "And you're like mine," Michael replied, the warmth between them evident. Later that night, after the lights went out and the orphanage fell quiet, Michael and Louie lay awake, their beds just a whisper apart. "Hey," Louie whispered, "let's stay up and talk about our plans. You know, the big dreams." Michael nodded. "Okay."

And so, in the darkness, the two boys stayed up late, quietly talking about their futures, the excitement of their dreams filling the room. Though their lives were far from easy, their friendship gave them hope that one day, things would change for the better.
"Hey Michael, do you want to marry a girl when you grow up?" Louie asked one evening. "No way! Girls are weird and gross," Michael replied with a grimace. "But Sofia is different. She's nice."
Louie nodded in agreement. "Yeah, she's cool."

It was Christmas Eve, and the orphanage bustled with its usual strict routine. The boys were in school, and Mr. Hagsworth announced, "You'll have a full week off for the holidays, but don't get too comfortable. We resume on January 2nd, and you'll be tested on everything we've learned. Today, we have an exam, and I hope you boys studied. You wouldn't want to make me angry, now would you?" Michael and Louie exchanged worried glances. They hadn't studied much, having stayed up late the night before, dreaming about their futures. Unsurprisingly, the exam didn't go well for them, and Mr. Hagsworth wasn't pleased. "You two are in trouble," he growled. "I'm telling Ms. Haasmaun."

At lunchtime, the boys were feeling the weight of their impending punishment. Suddenly, Frank, the resident bully, swaggered up to them with two other boys in tow. Frank was a chunky, pale-skinned kid with icy blue eyes and a cruel smirk. "How'd you do on your exam?" Frank taunted. "Let me guess—you failed! You two are nothing but dumb orphans, only good for playing baseball and listening to jazz."
"Back off, man!" Louie snapped. Frank laughed, shoving Louie. "Shut up, music man!"

In a flash, a fight broke out between the boys. Punches were thrown, and soon, a crowd gathered. Mr. Hagsworth stormed over and broke it up, but like always, he took Frank's side. "You boys are in big trouble now," Mr. Hagsworth sneered atMichael andLouie. When they returned to the orphanage that afternoon, Ms. Haasmaun was already waiting, her face twisted in anger. "I know what you two did at school. You're brats, ungrateful and stupid!" she shouted. "As punishment, you'll spend the rest of the day working around the living quarters. After that, you'll eat dinner alone, after all the other boys have finished, and you'll clean up after them too."
"But that's not fair!" Michael protested.
"Fair? I don't care about fair, you little brat.
I'm in charge here, not you," Ms. Haasmaun barked.
"And tomorrow, on Christmas Day, while the other boys enjoy their holiday, you'll be locked in your room and working."
"There'll be no Christmas for you," she added, her voice dripping with malice. Michael and Louie, exhausted and defeated, spent the evening doing chores. By the time they ate their lonely dinner, the joy of the season had all but disappeared.
"I wish something would happen to her," Michael muttered bitterly.
"She's like Krampus or something even worse."
Louie nodded. "Yeah, she's terrible."

Later that night, Sofia found the boys in the kitchen. "I saw what happened today," she whispered. "It's not fair, what she and that bully did to you. I don't like her either." Sofia smiled warmly at the boys and added, "Don't worry. I'll make sure you two have a Christmas present, and Ms. Haasmaun will never know." She said goodnight, promising to see them the next day. As they cleaned up and got ready for bed, Michael and Louie couldn't shake the feeling that something magical might be coming their way.

The Enchanted Visitor It was midnight when a cold breeze swept through the room. Michael and Louie stirred, their eyes fluttering open. The windows creaked, and another icy breeze filled the room before they mysteriously closed. Suddenly, shimmering white sparkles floated down from the ceiling, and before their astonished eyes, a woman appeared. She wore a regal white fur hat and coat adorned with silver and blue trimmings, and her dress shoes shimmered with silvery-blue hues. Her sky-blue eyes sparkled under silvery-blonde hair, and her face and hands gleamed with an ethereal, glimmery light.

"Who are you?" Michael asked, his voice full of awe.

"I am Frostine," the woman replied with a warm smile.

"I'm here to take you to a magical, wintry wonderland. You'll meet the King and Queen, and see things you've never imagined." The boys' eyes widened. "The King and Queen?" Louie exclaimed.

Frostine nodded. "Yes, but dress warmly. You'll need it where we're going." With a flick of her wrist, she pulled out a pouch of glistening sand and sprinkled it over herself and the boys. In the blink of an eye, they found themselves standing on a vast train platform, made of green, red, and white marble. A majestic train pulled up with a loud whistle, billowing white steam into the frosty air.

The train itself was breathtaking—red, gold, and silver, with a grand black engine trimmed in gold. Frostine led the boys aboard, and they marveled at the plush blue and red seats, the red-and-gold walls, and the rich carpeting beneath their feet. The air smelled of peppermint and hot cocoa, filling them with a sense of warmth and wonder.

As they settled into their seats, a conductor appeared, wearing a tall red-and-blue hat with golden buttons. "Welcome aboard! This train is bound for Snowkingdom, traveling near the North Pole. Sit back, relax, and enjoy the ride," he said with a friendly smile. A train waiter soon appeared, offering the boys hot chocolate topped with whipped cream and peppermint. The drink was rich and heavenly, unlike anything they had ever tasted.

They were also served a delicious meal of roast, potatoes with gravy, and their favorite vegetables. Dessert was a decadent chocolate ice cream with a candied cake, made with their favorite sweets—peppermints and bubble gum. Through the train's large windows, they watched the landscapes fly by—flatlands, rolling hills, serene beaches, peaceful pastures, dense forests, and towering mountains, all bathed in moonlight. Michael and Louie could hardly contain their excitement, their eyes wide with amazement.

As the train sped along, snow began to appear, sparkling under the moon. Ahead, glittering lights appeared on the horizon. The closer they got, the brighter and more magnificent the lights became. Michael and Louie exchanged wide-eyed glances, knowing they were about to enter the most beautiful city they had ever seen.

SNOWKINGDOM AWAITED

The train came to a halt at a grand station. Michael and Louie disembarked, arriving in Polaria, the capital of The Snow Kingdom. As they entered Polaria Central Station, they were greeted by a vibrant crowd clad in fur coats, hats, scarves, and an array of warm attire.

The inhabitants of the Snow Kingdom displayed an enchanting spectrum of colors—blues, pinks, greens, yellows, oranges, browns, and whites. Each person possessed unique pigment traits that defined their hue, making them strikingly beautiful. Men, women, and children filled the vast station, adorned with magnificent clocks and sparkling crystal chandeliers. The golden floors and glass walls embellished with colorful designs added to the station's grandeur, which surpassed even New York's Grand Central Station. Amid the bustling atmosphere, an announcement echoed through the loudspeakers: "Track 10 is leaving Polaria for Boston." Every holiday, children arrived in Polaria, having been personally selected by the King and Queen.

These children had never lived in the Snow Kingdom; only those born there had called it home for centuries. To those who visited, it became a cherished memory—a magical childhood dream, as Frostine described it. "The King and Queen have something for you, Michael, but you'll discover it when you meet them," said Frostine as they exited the vast train station. A round, red ruby car awaited them at the front, its plush white seats inviting. The driver, pale with striking green eyes, wore a ruby cap adorned with gold trimmings and a matching red suit. "Ahhh, the long-awaited child has finally arrived!" exclaimed the driver. Confused, Michael asked, "What do you mean?" "Wait and see," replied the driver with a chuckle. "All I can say is that you're a special little boy."

As they rode toward Crystal Palace, Michael and Louie gazed out in awe at the colorful residents of Polaria. People strolled with baby carriages, dogs, and shopping bags, while vibrant lights illuminated the buildings, crystals, and ice, creating a fairy-tale atmosphere.

Upon arriving at the magnificent Crystal Palace, both boys gasped in admiration. The palace glowed with a myriad of colors, captivating their imaginations. As they approached, a nobleman greeted them, saying, "You boys are in for a treat; you will meet our King and Queen."
As they walked through the palace, Michael, Louie, Frostine, and the nobleman marveled at the crystal and ice sculptures, chandeliers, and the lively activity around them. They finally arrived at a grand hall where King Rufus and Queen Pola sat majestically on their thrones. A door guard ushered them in. "Michael and Louie, this is King Rufus and Queen Pola," the nobleman announced. The boys stood in awe. King Rufus wore a stunning robe of blue, silver, and white, his face as pale as snow, with dark icy blue eyes and shimmering silver-blue hair. His robe was adorned with white fur and a rainbow of sparkling jewels, including rubies, sapphires, and emeralds, complemented by elegant white and silver attire.

Queen Pola, radiant with a glittering white complexion, had deep dark icy blue eyes surrounded by silver and blue sparkles. Her gown sparkled in blue, white, and silver, with long flowing sleeves, and her shoes gleamed in silver. With crowns of gold and embellished with sapphires, the King and Queen approached Michael and Louie warmly. "Hello, boys! We're so grateful to have you here. You are very special," said Pola with a smile. "Are you happy to see us?" asked Rufus. "We love it here; it's beautiful and magical!" exclaimed the boys in unison. "Everyone is so colorful, happy, and kind!" added Michael. "I feel like I'm dreaming," Louie remarked. "No, dear," replied Pola gently. "You're in the Snow Kingdom, in Polaria, the capital." She explained, "Michael and Louie, you are here to help us with a special mission.

We need your courage against a wicked man named Sumeron, who resides in a hot mountain just outside the Snow Kingdom. He plans to melt our realm on Christmas Day using a powerful array of mirrors that will focus the sun's rays upon us." Describing Sumeron as a miserable figure with goblins at his command, Rufus painted a grim picture. The goblins, dressed in red and orange, were not pleasant to behold. Sumeron, a tall man with jet-black hair and a wicked demeanor, sought to take over the Snow Kingdom and plunge it into darkness.

"There's only one thing that can stop him," Rufus said, producing a small dark blue velvet pouch filled with sparkling dust. "This magic dust must be used to destroy his mirrors and thwart his plans." Handing the pouch to Michael, Pola urged, "You must do this; no one else here has the courage." With determination, the boys declared, "We'll stop Sumeron and save the Snow Kingdom!" Queen Pola smiled, assuring them they would be heroes. The nobleman then promised to guide them to Sumeron's lair, and the King and Queen waved goodbye as the boys set off.

As they approached the intimidating mountain, the nobleman warned them about the goblins. Clad in their red and orange work suits, the goblins spotted the boys and gave chase. They ran until they reached Sumeron's lair, where one of the goblins seized Michael, who held the pouch of magical dust.

Brought before Sumeron, they saw his cruel throne surrounded by fire pits and his mirror machine. Sumeron, with a sinister smile, taunted them, calling them unwanted orphans and declaring his intent to enslave them after melting the Snow Kingdom. "You will never defeat me!" he sneered.
"No, we won't let you!" shouted Michael and Louie defiantly. Sumeron ensnared them in a net, but the nobleman stayed hidden, contemplating a rescue. A goblin named Hoppet approached him, expressing his desire to rebel against Sumeron's tyranny. He longed to return to his family and wished to help. "Of course, you can assist us," said the nobleman. When Sumeron left, Hoppet used a knife to cut the net and free the boys. With newfound determination, Michael and Louie raced to Sumeron's machine.

As they placed the magic dust inside, they declared, "Long live the Snow Kingdom forever!" They knew they had to escape quickly. Just then, the nobleman urged them to run as the machine would soon explode.
They bolted out just in time to hear Sumeron's furious scream. From a safe distance, they watched as the machine and part of the mountain erupted in a fiery explosion.

Returning triumphantly to Polaria, Michael and Louie were met with cheers and celebration. "You boys are heroes for saving the Snow Kingdom!" proclaimed King Rufus. "Now, let's clean you up and celebrate!"
"I have an announcement," Rufus continued. "When you grow up, you both will become kings of the Snow Kingdom." Astonished, the boys exclaimed, "Wait, what?" "Yes," Rufus affirmed. "Wow!" gasped Michael and Louie,

their eyes wide with wonder. The scene shifted to a grand sledding celebration through the streets of Polaria, where they joined King Rufus, Queen Pola, Frostine, the nobleman, and Hoppet, who had earned the nickname "The Good Goblin." Suddenly, Michael and Louie awoke in their beds at the orphanage on Christmas morning in 1950. "What a dream!" they exclaimed in unison, hopping out of bed and sneaking into the living room. "Merry Christmas! You boys have presents to open!" greeted Sophia with a beaming smile. "What happened to Ms. Haasmaun and Mr. Hagsworth?" asked Michael.

"They've been dismissed," Sophia replied.

"The city discovered their wrongdoings, and they'll face consequences for the money they stole from the orphanage."

"That's wonderful news!" shouted Michael and Louie in delight.

"We have a new head, Mr. Wrighton," Sophia added. "Merry Christmas, everyone!"

Michael then discovered a beautifully wrapped present beneath the tree—a Queen Pola doll in a fancy box. "Oh, it's stunning! I love it!" he exclaimed. Sophia wondered aloud where it had come from. They soon found a King Rufus doll, a charming train set, and shiny white shoes for each of them. That Christmas was filled with joy, laughter, and a sense of magic. Michael and Louie knew in their hearts where their gifts had come from. They were eventually adopted by Sophia, embarking on a happy childhood, destined to become the kings of the Snow Kingdom.

www.ingramcontent.com/pod-product-compliance
Lightning Source LLC
LaVergne TN
LVHW020954280125
802364LV00015B/1008